Sunni & Her Hip Hop Bunny

Earth Day Every Day

Lucy Ra'oof and Ashia Duprey

Vol. 1

Sunni Unlimited Media
www.sunniunlimitedmedia.com

First published by 3G Publishing, Inc., April, 2015.

Printed in the United States of America

ISBN: 978-1-941247-11-2

Illustrations by: Allison Conway and Fei Xu

This story was inspired by Sunni Grace Mauldin, a little girl who loved her blankie.

Special acknowledgements to the following individuals who saw our vision and helped us move full "STEAM" ahead: Wendy Newberry-Smith, TJ Williams, Darren Foreman, and Platinum recording Hip-Hop artist, "Da Brat," for her musical contributions.

Early one morning, not so long ago, my new hip hop bunny showed up at my home. Clothes made from my blankie that I had outgrown, with a sprinkle of magic and perfectly sewn.

On the day that we met, I had begun to fret because the school Earth Day Fair was real soon. Though the project was clear, I was just filled with fear that I was headed for show and tell doom.

When I asked my brother DJ, where I should begin, with a nod of his headphones and a shy little grin, he said, "That's one competition I don't think you can win."

For the school earth day fair I was supposed to share a single item or collection, to show environmental protection.

Then I heard this really cool beat, the rhythmic sound of bunny feet, and a voice with a smooth hip hop flair!

"My name is Steamy, nice to meet you Sunni! I am the world's first scientist and hip hop bunny! I have a little secret to share with you, there is nothing in this world that you can't do! Using research and STEAM you'll be on the right path with Science, Technology, Engineering, Arts and Math."

While the beat filled my head I moved from side to side, and Steamy's rhyme took us on a lyrical ride.

Steam is Cool, Steam is Fun
Steam is Great for Everyone
With a Hip and a Hop, a Heeeyyy and a Hooooo
Step to the Front, and Away we Gooooo!!!!

When we came to a stop we were in a magical land, with every resource you can imagine at hand. Then Steamy spun around with his hands in the air. He was smooth, he was cool, he had style and flair!

13

He said, "The environment is the world that we all must share, so for show and tell, simply show that you care."

Before you throw things away, please make sure that they are trash!

Can we reuse a string for a belt or a sash?

Then with a wink, Steamy said, "think about it Sunni,

can paper be recycled to make new money,

or can a blankie make clothes for a magical bunny?"

Recycling prevents waste and turns old into new, saving useful materials that we can reuse!!

Be sure to recycle, just give it a try, it protects our world from the grass to the sky. Recycling is cool, it is hip, it is smart, it is something we ALL can do from our hearts!

With a Hip and a Hop, a Heeeyyy and a Hooooo
Step to the front and away we Gooooo!!!

My friend Steamy is so unique! He's the coolest math, science and technology geek. Whenever I have a problem he always appears, so no need to worry or shed any tears!

Now I get it and I know what to do, recycle to make a guitar for school! With a bowl, rubber bands and some cardboard, I'll make a guitar that gets a top score.

I will always remember to do my part, to choose the 3Rs right from the start. To Recycle, Reuse and Reduce everyday will save our planet in a loving way.

My bunny Steamy is so smart and kind, he helps me research and expand my mind. He is savvy, he is cool, and incredibly rare. With his help I won 1st place at the Earth Day Fair!

So now you know that I did my best, and that my guitar was a huge success. DJ was there to see me win, with a big high 5 and a great big grin!

Sunni's
Lab Book

Earth Day Project

Problem (Question):

What is a single item or collection that shows environmental protection?

Research:

3Rs: Recycle, Reuse, Reduce

Recycling prevents waste and turns old into new. It is saving useful materials that we can reuse.

Earth Day is the Earth's birthday.

Earth Day began on April 22, 1970. Over 100 countries celebrate the planet on this day to show environmental protection.

Hypothesis (Prediction):

A guitar made from recycled materials will show environmental protection.

Materials:
Bowl, rubber bands, cardboard packing box, glue, tape, scissors, markers, and a plastic bread tie.

Experiment (Method): Guitar Using Packing Box:

1. Wrap rubber bands around the bowl and tape in place.

2. Trace the shape of a guitar on two sides of a large packing box and cut out.

3. Decorate the guitar cut outs.

4. Use the same bowl to trace and cut a circle in the center of one of the cut outs.

5. Tape or glue the bowl to the back of the cut out that has the hole in the center.

6. Attach the second cut out to the back of the bowl.

7. Use the plastic bread tie to play guitar.

Conclusion (Results):
Everyday materials can be reused to make something new like my new guitar. The 3Rs (Recycle, Reuse, Reduce) are key to saving the planet. Earth Day is Every Day!

Sunni &

www.ingramcontent.com/pod-product-compliance
Lightning Source LLC
Chambersburg PA
CBHW041134170626
46815CB00009B/356